BADGER'S
PARTING GIFTS

BADGER'S
PARTING GIFTS

Susan Varley

HarperCollins *Children's Books*

To my tutors

First published in hardback in Great Britain by Andersen Press Ltd in 1984
First published in paperback by Picture Lions in 1985
Re-issued in paperback by Picture Lions in 1992
This edition published by Collins Picture Books in 2002

1 3 5 7 9 10 8 6 4 2

ISBN-13: 978-0-00-784745-7

Picture Lions and Collins Picture Books are imprints of the Children's Division, part of
HarperCollins Publishers Ltd.

Text and illustrations copyright © Susan Varley 1984
The author/illustrator asserts the moral right to be identified as the author/illustrator of the work.

Printed and bound in China

Badger was dependable, reliable, and always ready to lend a helping paw. He was also very old, and he knew almost everything. Badger was so old that he knew he must soon die.

Badger wasn't afraid of death. Dying meant only that he would leave his body behind and, as his body didn't work as well as it had in days gone by, Badger wasn't too concerned about that. His only worry was how his friends would feel when he was gone. Hoping to prepare them, Badger had told them that someday soon he would be going down the Long Tunnel, and he hoped they wouldn't be too sad when it happened.

One day, as Badger was watching Mole and Frog race down the hillside, he felt especially old and tired. He wished more than anything that he could run with them, but he knew his old legs wouldn't let him. He watched Mole and Frog for a long time, enjoying the sight of his friends having a good time.

It was late when he arrived home. He wished the moon good night and closed the curtains on the cold world outside. He made his way slowly down to the warm fire that was waiting for him deep underground.

He had his supper and then sat down at his desk to write a letter. When he had finished, he settled down in his rocking chair near the fire. He gently rocked himself to and fro and soon was fast asleep having a strange yet wonderful dream like none he'd ever had before.

Much to Badger's surprise, he was running. Ahead of him was a very long tunnel. His legs felt strong and sure as he ran towards it. He no longer needed his walking stick, so he left it lying on the floor of the tunnel. Badger moved swiftly, running faster and faster through the long passageway, until his paws no longer touched the earth. He felt himself turning head over paws, falling and tumbling, but nothing hurt. He felt free. It was as if he had fallen out of his body.

The following day Badger's friends gathered anxiously outside Badger's door. They were worried because he hadn't come out to say good morning as he always did.

Fox broke the sad news that Badger was dead and read Badger's note to them. It said simply, "Gone down the Long Tunnel. Bye Bye, Badger."

All the animals had loved Badger, and everyone was very sad. Mole especially felt lost, alone and desperately unhappy.

In bed that night Mole could think only of Badger. Tears rolled down his velvety nose, soaking the blankets he clung to for comfort.

Outside, it began to snow. Winter had begun, and soon a thick layer of snow hid the animals' homes, where they would stay snug and warm during the cold months.

The snow covered the countryside, but it didn't conceal the sadness that Badger's friends felt.

Badger had always been there when anyone needed him. The animals all wondered what they would do now that he was gone. Badger had told them not to be unhappy, but it was hard not to be.

As spring drew near, the animals often visited each other and talked about the days when Badger was alive.

Mole was good at using scissors, and he told about the time Badger had taught him how to cut out a chain of moles from a piece of folded paper. Paper moles had littered the ground that day. Mole remembered the joy he'd felt when he had finally succeeded in making a complete chain of moles with all the paws joined.

Frog was an excellent skater. He recalled how Badger had helped him take his first slippery steps on the ice. Badger had gently guided him across the ice until he had gained enough confidence to glide out on his own.

Fox remembered how, when he was a young cub, he could never knot his tie properly until Badger showed him how.

"Starting with the wide end of the tie, it's right over left, once around to the back, up, then down through the crossover and, holding the back of the tie, push the knot up to the neck."

Fox could now tie every knot ever invented and some he'd made up himself. And of course his own necktie was always perfectly knotted.

Badger had given Mrs Rabbit his special recipe for gingerbread and had shown her how to bake gingerbread rabbits. Mrs Rabbit was well known throughout the countryside for her excellent cooking. As she talked about her first cooking lesson with Badger, so long ago, she could almost smell the wonderful fragrance of gingerbread fresh from the oven.

Each of the animals had a special memory of Badger – something he had taught them that they could now do extremely well. He had given them each a parting gift to treasure always. Using these gifts they would be able to help each other.

As the last of the snow melted, so did the animals' sadness. Whenever Badger's name was mentioned, someone remembered another story that made them all smile.

One warm spring day as Mole was walking on the hillside where he'd last seen Badger, he wanted to thank his friend for his parting gift.

"Thank you, Badger," he said softly, believing that Badger would hear him.

And...somehow...Badger did.